The Spooky Tree

Written by Arthur Ruolo
Illustrated by Marilyn Mets

Published by McClanahan Book Companay, Inc.
23 West 26th Street, New York, NY 10010
ISBN: 1-56293-944-0
LCC: 97-71832
Printed in the U.S.A.

When Liz and I moved into our new house, we liked everything about it—except for one tree in the yard.

It had long, twisty branches and weird, dark leaves. One side looked like a spooky face.

It was a spooky tree.

Most of the time the tree just stood there.

But at night it waved its long, twisty branches
and made spooky shadows on my wall.

When we played baseball, nobody used the spooky tree for third base.

And nobody hid behind it during hide-and-seek.

Liz and I didn't like the spooky tree—and that was that. I wanted Dad to cut it down.

But Dad said, "Why, Billy? It's a good tree, so big and strong."

"Big and strong and spooky," I thought.

One day our baseball got lost.

Liz and I went looking for it.

Suddenly Liz shouted,
"I found the ball! And I think the
spooky tree winked at me!"

I didn't wait to see it wink again. I just ran
away as fast as I could.

In the middle of
the night a thunderstorm
woke us up.

A big bolt of lightning struck a pole and sent it crashing down right toward our house!

But all of a sudden it stopped. The spooky tree had caught the pole—and saved our house.

Then I had to agree with Dad. The spooky tree was a good tree.

The next time we played baseball, Liz made the tree third base.

It became my
favorite hiding place.

On Halloween, when
Liz and I got dressed up . . .

so did the spooky tree.

Now the tree watches over our house every night.
And you know what? It doesn't look spooky anymore.
It is our friend.